W9-CQJ-109

For BRAYDEN
I'm Loves You.
Jan. 30, 2014.
xxooxx

Monster League Baseball
presents

Monster at the Bat

By Hal Pollock

A Publication of Milk & Cookies Press

1230 Park Avenue
New York, New York 10128
Tel: 212-427-7139 • Fax: 212-860-8852
bricktower@aol.com • www.BrickTowerPress.com

Library of Congress Cataloging-in-Publication Data

Pollock, Hal
Ron Borresen
ISBN-13: 978-1-59687-884-6
ISBN-10: 1-59687-884-3
Library of Congress Control Number: 2009922637
Juvenile Fiction, Family/Siblings

10 9 8 7 6 5 4 3 2 1

Monster League Baseball
presents

Monster
at the Bat

By Hal Pollock

Milk & Cookies Press, Publishers

WELCOME TO
MONSTERVILLE

It was early one clear morning
When I looked up in the sky,
And I could swear I saw
A tiny baseball whizzing by.

"Can't be," I said to no one there,
"A ball in outer space?"
Then I recalled the legend
And a smile came to my face.

In the ancient town of Monsterville,
You'll hear it constantly;
The story of the greatest game
In monster history.

Back when Titans took the field
On diamonds ever green,
With fabled teams and players,
The best there's ever been.

There were Creatures from Horrendo,
And Zombies from Cape Dead,
The Horror Town Unspeakables,
And Devils from New Dread.

And then came the Demon Dogs,
The team from Pitchfork Downs,
Champions for six straight years.
No one could take their crowns.

Their pitchers slobbered on the ball.
They never gave up hits.
Their Great Danes in the outfield
Plastered glue upon their mitts.

And when the Demons came to bat
The hits came one by one.
And once upon the bases,
Oh, how those dogs could run.

Here was a team to root for,
This stalwart monster troop.
They did us proud in Monsterville,
An oddly handsome group.

There was Chowderhead and Phungo,
Wee Bobby Bugster too,
Frankenberg and Dragon,
Uglies in the bullpen crew.

Frankenberg

Phungo

Dragon

Chowderhead

Wee Bobby Bugster

On the bench was Flopster,
And pitch-hitter Gnarly Nate,
With Skinny Slimeball on the mound,
And Gash behind the plate.

Flopster

Skinny Slimeball

Gnarly
Nate

Uglies

Gash

The star, of course, was Mongo,
First of the slugging rank.
More homers to his credit
Than Barry, Babe, or Hank.

His muscles looked like mountains;
His bat, a large oak tree.
He terrified the pitchers
'Cause he swung so viciously.

Beloved by little monsters,
Adored throughout the town,
Mongo was the hero
For a hundred miles around.

Fine team by any measure,
All good players, tried and true;
But to win the Monster Series
Was the thing they could not do.

"Wait 'till next year," was the cry
That finally came to pass,
When our Monsters made the Series
Against the Demon Dogs at last.

Oh, how the Monstervilleans
Had waited, one and all.
Their hated rivals had arrived.
"Let's go! Come on! Play ball!"

Now the Demons had a pitcher
By the name of Bark McChew,
The meanest fiend upon the mound
The Monsters ever knew.

With a windup like a windmill
And a pair of laser eyes,
He could throw the ball with either paw,
His pitches to disguise.

The Series was dead even.
The games stood three and three.
The final game would tell the tale
Of who the best would be.

Eight innings on, our team was flat.
The Demons had their way.
The score stood three to nothing
With one inning left to play.

When Frankenberg went swinging
And Dragon did the same,
A sadly silence fell upon
The fans there at the game.

Fair-weathered few departed.
The rest stayed where they sat,
Hoping that Great Mongo
Would get one more whack at bat.

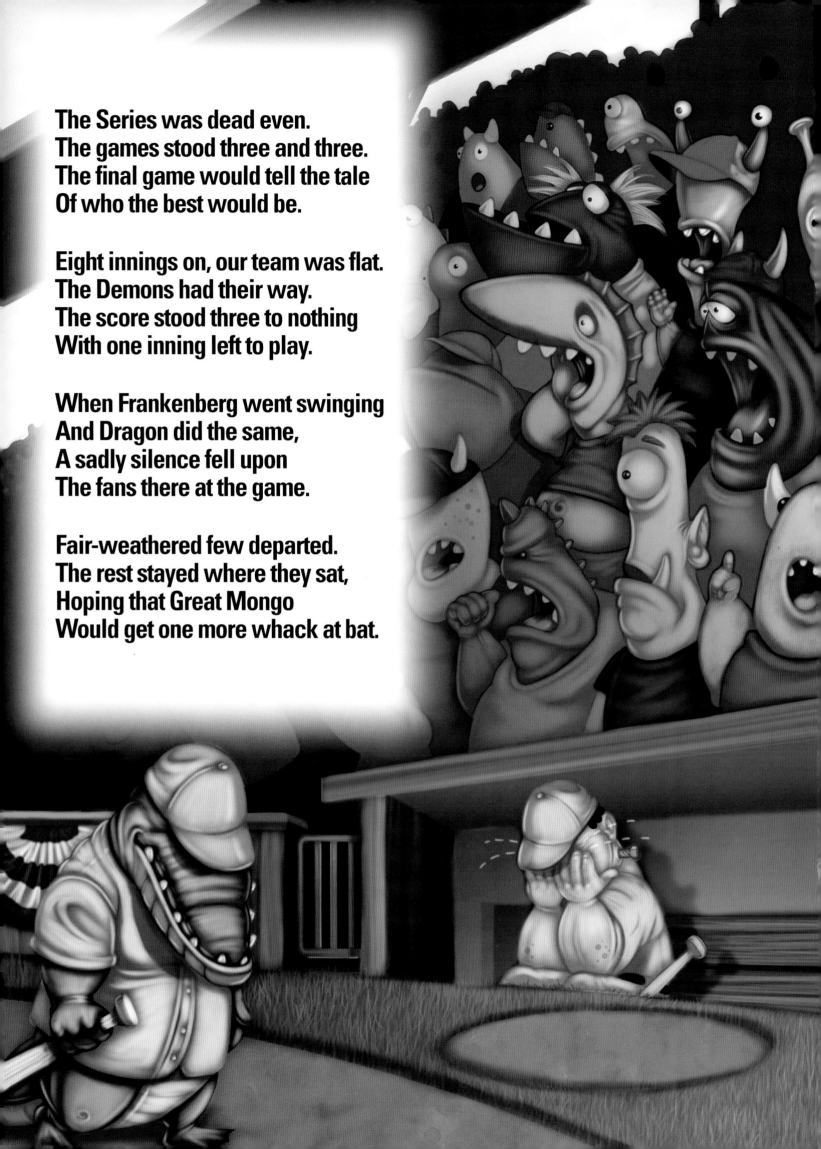

First Chowderhead, then Four Eyes,
And Bugster after him,
So Mongo's chance to see a pitch
Was looking very grim.

But Chowder came up to the plate
and leaned into the ball.
It grazed across his uniform,
And then we heard the call.

"Take first!" the umpire shouted,
Brushing dirt from Chowder's knees.
The plump one picked himself back up
And glided down with ease.

Then Philly Four Eyes took his turn,
Laid down a perfect bunt,
Slid two heads first into the base.
Was really quite a stunt.

"Safe!" the umpire bellowed
As the crowd cried out with glee.
Two were down and two were on,
But we still needed three.

Up came Bobby Bugster,
As Mongo strolled on deck,
Cool and calm as he could be,
And Bob a nervous wreck.

He stood there scared half silly
For good reason, I suppose.
Barky scotched him twice before,
Once right upon the nose.

McChew took aim at Bobby,
And he tried to knock him flat.
When Bobby hit the dirt to duck,
The ball bounced off his bat.

It squiggled through the infield
Just beyond the shortstop's mitt,
Came to rest on outfield grass,
A seeing eyeball hit.

And when the dust had settled
The crowd exploded in a roar.
A monster stood at every base
With Mongo knocking at the door.

The ballpark was electric.
The drama was all that.
Game and title on the line,
Mighty Mongo at the bat.

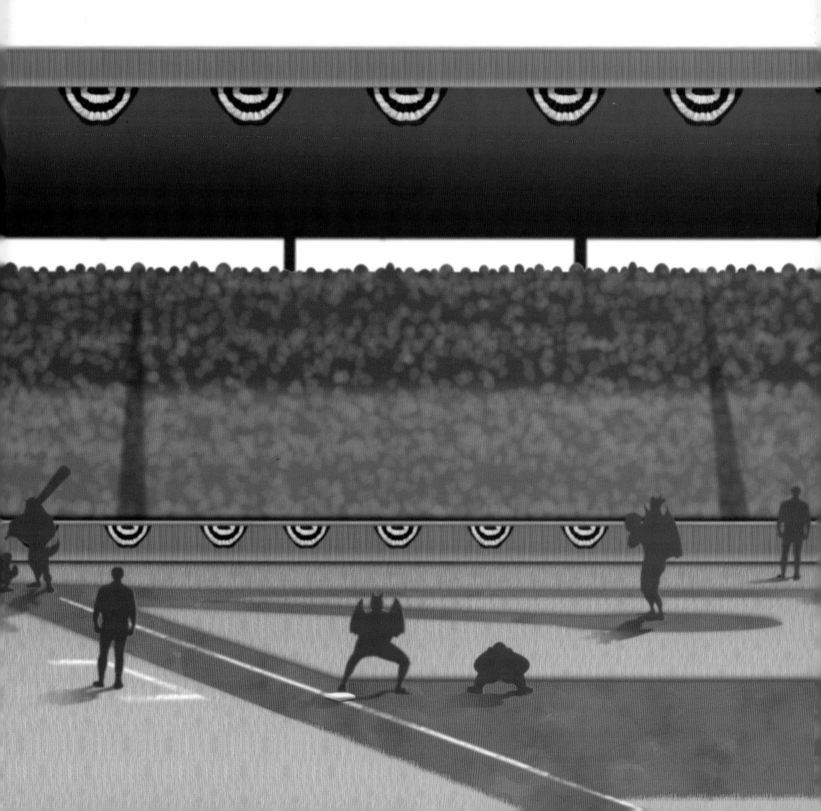

Flopster stood atop the dugout
Waving both his ears,
Whipped the crowd into a frenzy.
Mongo heard their lusty cheers.

He gazed out at the scoreboard,
And he pointed with his bat
As if to say, "You see that thing?
I'm aiming over that."

Bark fired off a screwball
Like a bullet from a gun.
Mongo stood there motionless
The umpire called, "Strike one!"

"No!" screamed out the angry crowd,
"A strike it cannot be!
It missed the plate by half a mile!
The umpire cannot see!"

Then Bark unleashed a curveball.
It came straight out of the blue,
Curling ten feet to the left.
The umpire cried, "Strike two!"

"Kill him! Kill the umpire!"
Someone shouted from the crowd.
There could have been a riot
Had not Mongo said out loud,

"Don't worry 'bout a strike or two.
It doesn't bother me.
He'll have to offer one more yet
Before the call's strike three."

Then Bark let fly the fastest ball
That eyes had ever seen,
Came rushing at the speed of light
A white-hot jellybean.

Mongo dared not let it pass him.
He swung with all his might.
His oak tree whooshed right through the air
To meet the sphere of white.

Every voice fell silent.
All hearts then skipped a beat.
The hopes and dreams of Monsterville
Were laid at Mongo's feet.

There was a flash like lightning,
A thunder sound like ne'er before,
As Mongo cracked the hapless ball
And crushed it to the core.

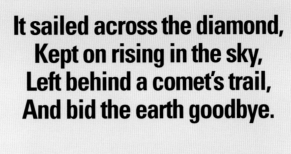

It sailed across the diamond,
Kept on rising in the sky,
Left behind a comet's trail,
And bid the earth goodbye.

And yes, it kept on soaring
Onward, upward to the sun.
The greatest slam in history,
A monster-ous home run!

Mongo circled 'round the bases
As he lightly doffed his hat.
A hero for all ages,
Now our Mongo was all that.

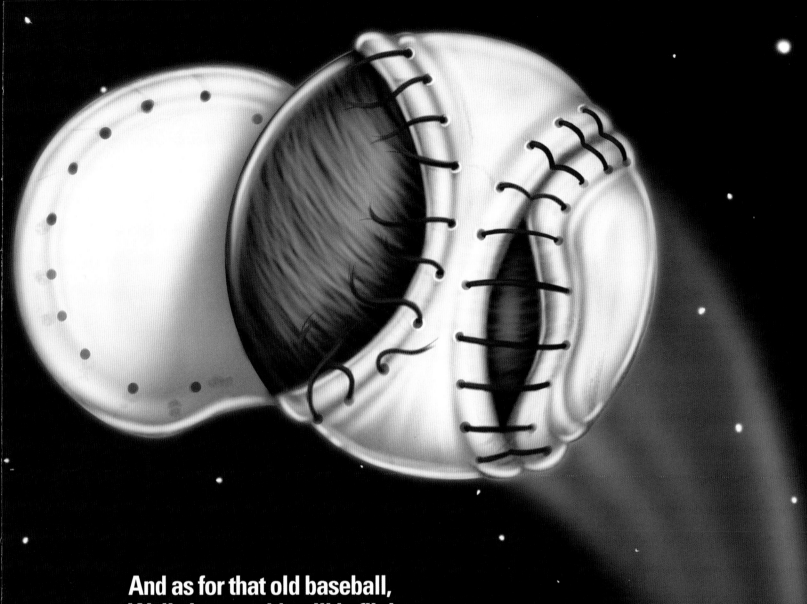

And as for that old baseball,
Well, they say it's still in flight.
And sometimes you can see it
In the early morning light.

It orbits far around the sun
Then travels back again.
Perhaps one day you'll see it,
But you never know just when.

A tiny speck against the sky,
So open your eyes wide
To see the famous satellite
Of stitches and horsehide.

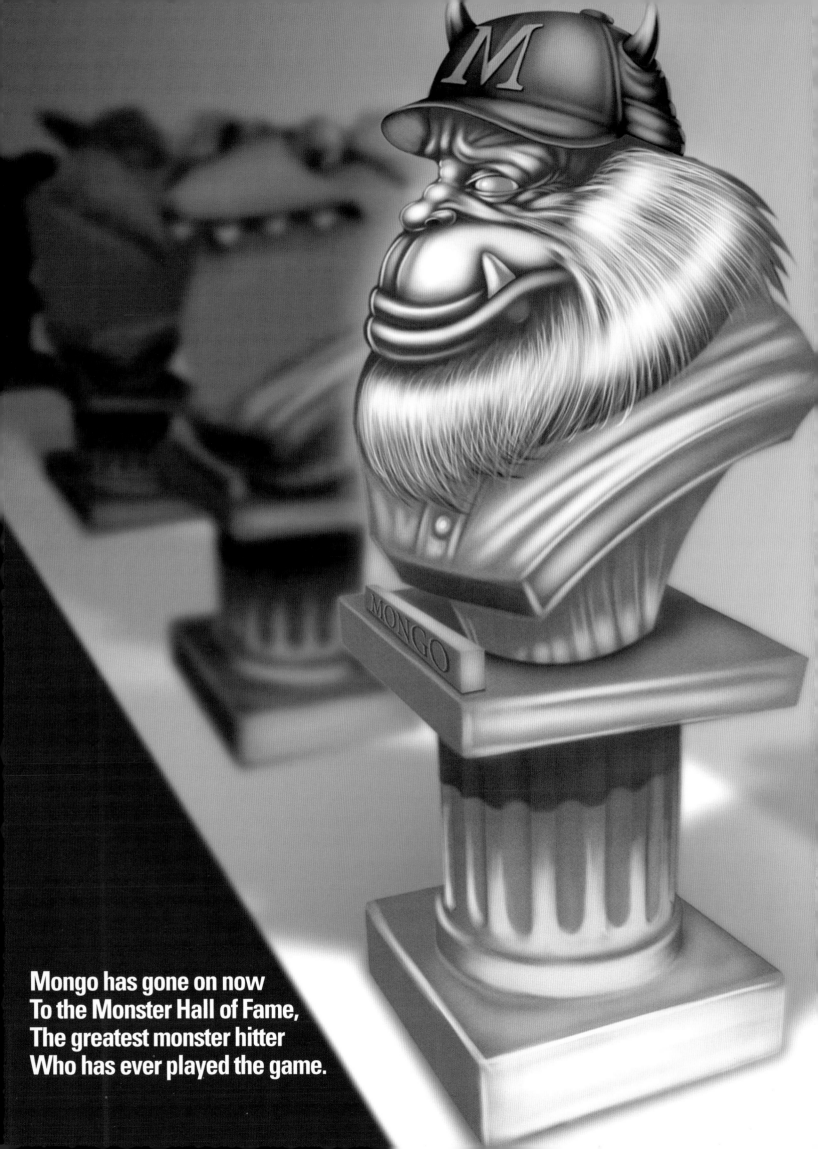

Mongo has gone on now
To the Monster Hall of Fame,
The greatest monster hitter
Who has ever played the game.

And somewhere in the heavens
Surely Mongo's smiling still,
Glad to see that once again
There's joy in Monsterville.

For sales, editorial information, subsidiary rights information
or a catalog, please write or phone or e-mail

Milk & Cookies Press
1230 Park Avenue
New York, New York 10128, US
Sales: 1-800-68-BRICK
Tel: 212-427-7139 Fax: 212-860-8852
www.bricktowerpress.com
email: bricktower@aol.com.

For sales in the United States, please contact
National Book Network
nbnbooks.com
Orders: 800-462-6420
Fax: 800-338-4550
custserv@nbnbooks.com

For sales in the UK and Europe please contact our
distributor, Gazelle Book Services
Falcon House, Queens Square
Lancaster, LA1 1RN, UK
Tel: (01524) 68765 Fax: (01524) 63232
email: gazelle4go@aol.com.

For Australian and New Zealand sales please contact
Bookwise International
174 Cormack Road, Wingfield, 5013, South Australia
Tel: 61 (0) 419 340056 Fax: 61 (0)8 8268 1010
email: karen.emmerson@bookwise.com.au